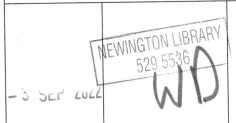

WELCOME,
STUDENTS!

—TANK CAR—

AND LAST BUT NOT LEAST ...
—CABOOSE!—

Dedicated to Teddy Schupack
A. K. R.

For my mother
M. Y.

First published 2020 by Walker Books Ltd
87 Vauxhall Walk, London SE11 5HJ

2 4 6 8 10 9 7 5 3 1

Text © 2020 Amy Krouse Rosenthal
Illustrations © 2020 Mike Yamada

The right of Amy Krouse Rosenthal and Mike Yamada to be identified as the author and illustrator respectively of this work has been asserted by them in accordance with the Copyright, Designs and Patents Act 1988

This book has been typeset in Grenadine MVB Medium

Printed in China

British Library Cataloguing in Publication Data:
a catalogue record for this book is available from the British Library

ISBN 978-1-4063-8613-4

www.walker.co.uk

CHOO-CHOO SCHOOL

WELCOME STUDENTS

Gg Hh Pp

1, 2, 3,
4, 5, 6, 7,
Freight!

Amy Krouse Rosenthal   illustrated by Mike Yamada

WALKER BOOKS
AND SUBSIDIARIES
LONDON · BOSTON · SYDNEY · AUCKLAND

Good morning! Good morning!
All aboard the train school run.

Next stop is Choo-Choo School.
Come on, everyone!

We're greeted as we pull in:
"Welcome to the day!"

And the Head Teacher calls out,
"No racing in the haul-way!"

Teacher takes his place up front.
He helps us stay on track.

Most of us like middle spots,
But Caboose works best in back.

First we recite the classroom rules:
"Work hard, play fair, be kind."

Then Teacher asks excitedly,
"Are you ready to train your minds?"

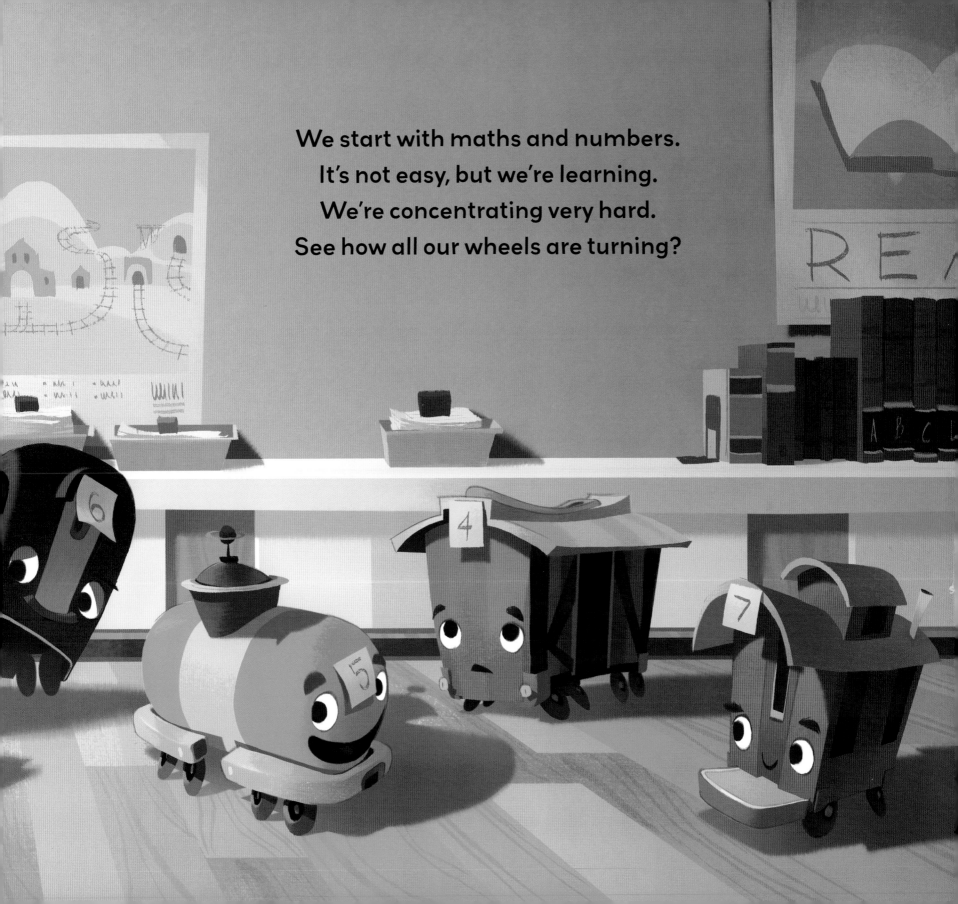

We start with maths and numbers.
It's not easy, but we're learning.
We're concentrating very hard.
See how all our wheels are turning?

Teacher signals to the clock.
"It's ten fifteen!" we chime.

We zoom to our next station.
(Trains like to be on time.)

In P.E. we practise climbing.
We work together as a team.

"Chugga-chugga-choo YAHOO!"

It feels good to blow off steam.

We fly through a long tunnel.
"It's dusty," Flatcar wheezes.
Boxcar is at the ready
Whenever someone sneezes.

"Ah-choo-choo!"

Now everyone is thirsty.
Tank Car has loads of juice.
We take turns wetting our whistles.
"I'm always last!" whines Caboose.

Lunch is always so much fun.
Diner loves to entertain.
"What do you call us now?" he jokes.
"A chew-chew choo-choo train!"

After lunch, we go to music.
Conductor leads us all in song.
Flatcar sings a bit off-key.
We just smile and hum along.

We're learning the whole alphabet.
We've gotten pretty far.
Do we have a favourite yet?
Of course! The letter *R*!

Sleeper dozes off in class.
His snores are quite a hoot.
We know just how to wake him:
"On the count of three...

Toot toot!"

When the final whistle blows,
We put everything away.

Time to rest so we'll be pumped
For another day at Choo-Choo School!